FOR THE GOEBBERT FAMILY-

A circle of strength, founded on faith...joined in love...kept by God.

-DS

www.mascotbooks.com

THE PUMPKIN EATING DINOSAUR!

Fourth Printing. This Mascot Books edition printed in 2022.

For more information, please contact:
Mascot Books, an imprint of Amplify Publishing Group
620 Herndon Parkway #320
Herndon, VA 20170
info@mascotbooks.com

Library of Congress Control Number: 2019905274

CPSIA Code: PRT0521D
ISBN-13: 978-1-64543-044-5

Printed in the United States

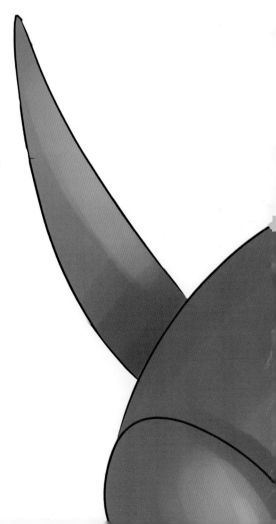

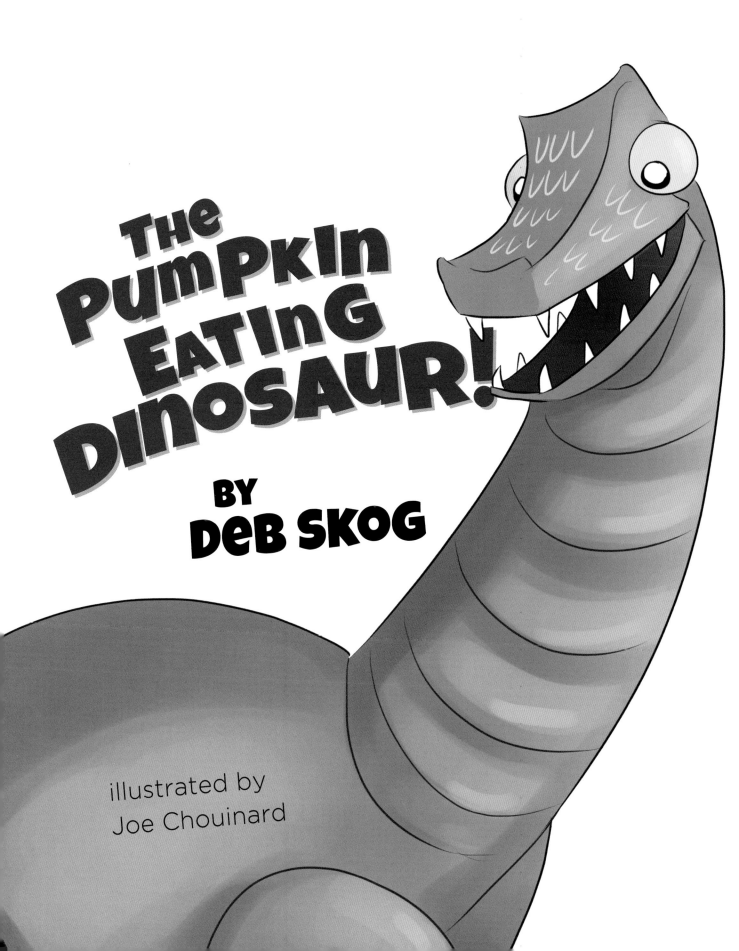

THE PUMPKIN EATING DINOSAUR!

BY DEB SKOG

illustrated by
Joe Chouinard

It's a beautiful fall day at Goebbert's Pumpkin Farm! The air is crisp and the sun is shining. Daniel, Trevor, and their mom and dad arrive at the farm, ready to see all the sights.

"Where should we go first?" Mom says. "I like to see all the animals and take the wagon ride out to the pumpkin patch."

"I love all the goodies in the market, like the homemade caramel apples and the famous hot apple cider donuts," Dad says.

But for Daniel and Trevor, there's only one spot for them—

The path to the Pumpkin Eating Dinosaur is lined with bright orange pumpkins, and the delicious scent of kettle corn and fresh hot apple cider donuts fills the air.

As they get closer, they see the dinosaur is asleep in his pen. "Listen!" says Daniel. "The Pumpkin Eating Dinosaur is snoring!"

Other children gather around, and together they chant, **"WAKE HIM UP! WAKE HIM UP!"**

Slowly, the dinosaur awakens. He rises up high above the children and greets them in his slow deep voice.

"GOOOOOD MOOORRRNNING!"

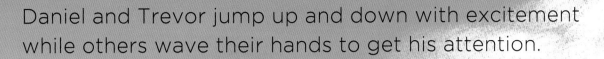

Daniel and Trevor jump up and down with excitement while others wave their hands to get his attention.

"CHOMP! CHOMP! CHOMP!

ROAR! ROAR! ROAR!

HE'S THE PUMPKIN EATING DINOSAUR!"

Trevor smiles and replies, "Hello!"

The Pumpkin Eating Dinosaur playfully blows some smoke at Trevor and lets him stroke his snout.

Next, he looks around to see which pumpkin he will eat today. There are so many to choose from! Will it be a big orange one, or a small green one?

Daniel and Trevor point out a big, bright orange pumpkin near them. "Pick this one, pick this one!" they shout.

The Pumpkin Eating Dinosaur spots their pumpkin and snags it with his sharp metal teeth! He slowly rises up with the big orange pumpkin in his jaws.

The kids all yell and chant:

"EAT IT! EAT IT! EAT IT!
CHOMP! CHOMP! CHOMP!
ROAR! ROAR! ROAR!

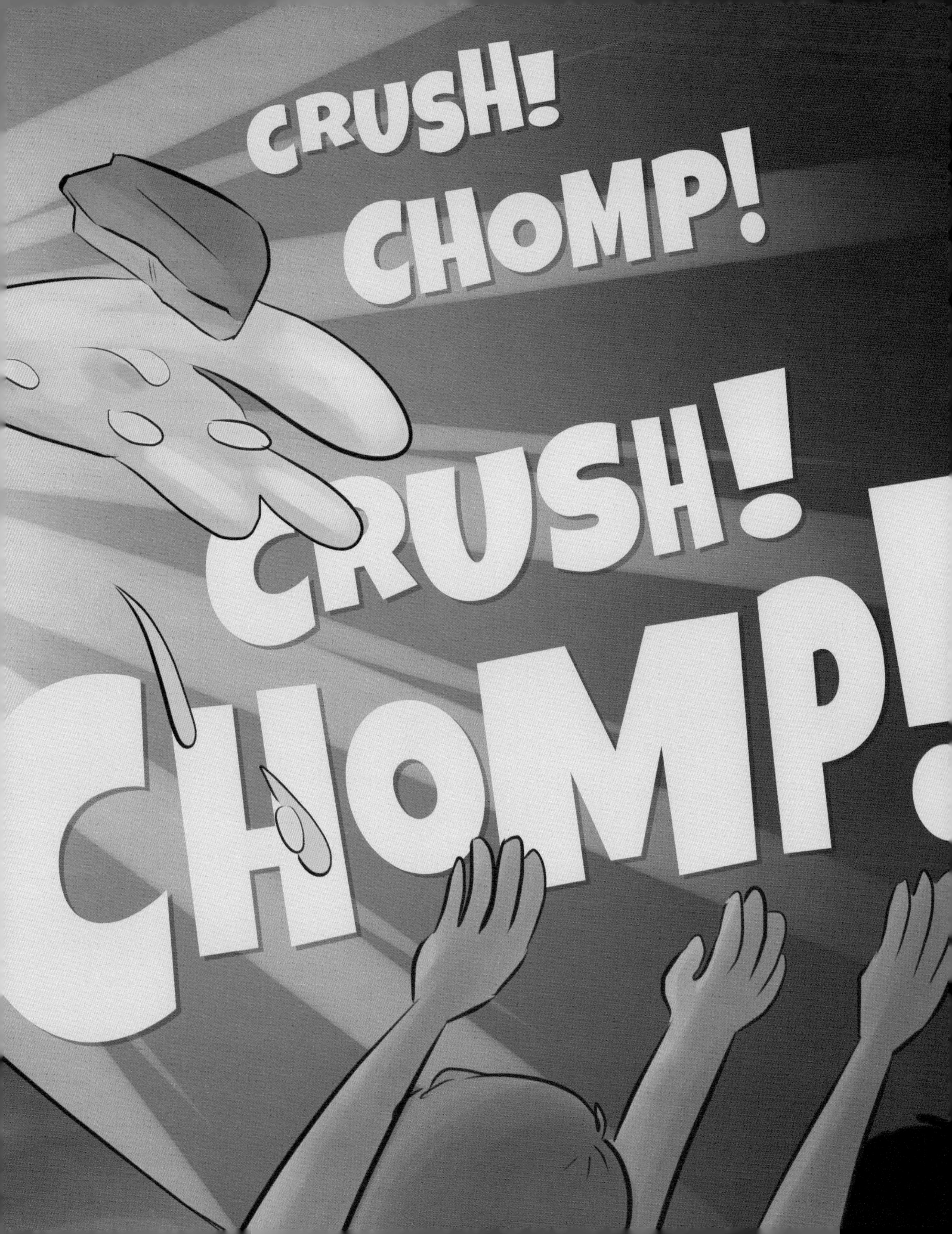
CRUSH!
CHOMP!
CRUSH!
CHOMP!

The Pumpkin Eating Dinosaur chomps and chomps on his snack and lets out a big

BUUuuURRRPpP!!!!!!!

"Excuuuuse me!" the Pumpkin Eating Dinosaur says. "Those pumpkins are tasty!"

The crowd claps and cheers as the Pumpkin Eating Dinosaur says, "GOODBYE!"

Trevor and his family wave to the dinosaur and say goodbye. Daniel yells out, "See you next fall!"

At the end of the day, the boys carry their pumpkins back to the car to take home. Dad has a dozen apple cider donuts as well.

"So boys," Mom asks. "What was the highlight of your day?"

The boys just smile at one another.

ABOUT THE AUTHOR

Deb is a retired kindergarten teacher who always loved to read and write. She received her master's degree in Education from University of Illinois.

Deb has been a dedicated friend and employee of the Goebbert family for many years.

Her first book, *The Pumpkin Eating Dinosaur*, as well as her second book, *A Day at the Pumpkin Farm*, and now her third book, *The Pumpkin Express*, all were inspired by her love for the farm. They reflect the joy it brings to so many who visit each year.

Her husband Jeff and adult children Zack, Sam, and Justin have always inspired her to pursue her dream of becoming an author.

With her strong faith she believes everything is possible with God.

I Can Do ALL THINGS Through
Christ Who Strengthens Me

Philippians 4:13